SATOSHI'S FABLES

THE MORAL OF THE BITCOIN STORY

BOB SEEMAN

ISBN: 9798840356975 (Paperback)
ISBN: 9798840357330 (Hardcover)

Publisher: CyberCurb, Vancouver. Author: Bob Seeman. The author has also published the foremost bitcoin-skeptic book, The Coinmen. Jack and the Beanstalk by Ciara Mahaffy. Cover design by CyberCurb. Most pictures by Milo Winter.

The Miner and the City People

A Miner was digging for gold and found pyrite that had a golden hue and was known as Fool's Gold.

The Miner didn't say the pyrite was gold, he said it was better than gold – a hedge against inflation and also "dig-it-all" gold.

City People believed him and he became filthy rich. The City People believed they were rich too.

The Country People did not believe him and spent their money instead on farming their land.

The City People ignored the Country People since they spoke "fear, uncertainty and doubt."

When inflation came, the country people had plenty to eat, but the city people starved.

Moral: All that glitters is not gold.

The City Person and the Farmers

One City Person was nobody's fool.

He bought the Fool's Gold and used it as collateral to ensure a stock of food delivery from the Farmers every week.

But when inflation came, the food from the Farmers stopped. Everyone had realised that the Fool's Gold was worthless.

Moral: Fool's Gold does not buy food.

The Goose and the Golden Egg

There was once a Farmer who possessed the most wonderful Goose you can imagine, for every day when he visited the nest, the Goose had laid a beautiful, glittering, golden egg.

The Farmer took the eggs to market and soon got very rich. But it was not long before he grew impatient with the Goose because she gave him only a single golden egg a day. He was not getting rich fast enough. So he got the idea of killing the Goose so he could get all her golden eggs immediately.

But, of course, there were no eggs in his poor dead Goose.

Moral: He who is greedy is always in want.

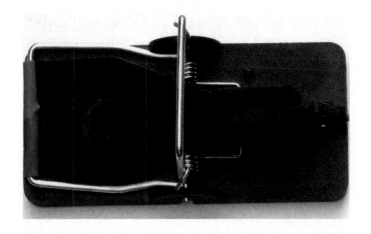

Two Mice and the House with the Mouse Traps

Jimmy and Kimmy were two Mice who lived in the house of Mr. Brown.

Mr. Brown didn't like mice so he set up mouse traps all over the house.

Jimmy was very good at getting at the cheese without getting caught in the trap. He got fatter and fatter and, therefore, slower and one day, alas, he was caught.

Kimmy didn't try for the cheese. He got thinner and thinner, but he stayed alive.

Moral: When a game is rigged, don't play.

The Young Man and the Swallow

A Young Man spent foolishly and was left with only the clothes on his back, and fine clothes they were because he had once been very rich.

When he looked up at the sky, a Swallow flew by. He rejoiced, "Now that the Swallows have come," he thought to himself, "can summer be far behind? I'll sell my sweaters, coat and hat and go to the gambling casino and soon I'll be rich again!"

So he sold everything except his shorts and sweat shirt and went off gambling.

But there was a sudden change in the weather and the temperature plunged. The poor guy froze.

Moral: One swallow does not a summer make.

It's How You Play the Game

Rover, Spot, Rosie, Scottie, and Bud were playing poker – not for money, but just to see who was top Dog.

They were also arguing because three of them said that winning at poker was all luck; everything depended on the hand you were dealt. But the other two (who were winning) said, "It's not the hand you're dealt. It's how you play the game!"

At the end, a top Dog emerged, but – as you can see in the picture – he was cheating.

Moral: When you don't know who the mark is, you're it.

Having Fun Is Good

"Throw caution to the winds," one Lady said to another, "have fun today, no matter the hangover tomorrow."

"The trouble is," the other Lady answered, "only a few are having fun. The rest of us are paying for it."

Moral: When one person wins, another should not have to lose.

The Pied Piper

Everyone knows the story of the Pied Piper. The town was full of rats and no one could get rid of them.

So the Town Councillors called in a Pied Piper who was said to play such enchanting tunes on his pipe that he could lure away all creatures, even rats.

The Piper came and he played so sweetly on his pipe that, sure enough, all the rats came out of their burrows and followed him away from the town and into the ocean where they all drowned.

"Hurrah," said the Town Councillors – but they hadn't noticed that the Piper's sweet music had also lured away all the town's children.

Moral: Watch out for unintended consequences.

The House of Cards by Chardin
(1699-1779)

The picture on the opposite page is one of four identified versions of The House of Cards painted by Chardin.

A house of cards, was a common theme in paintings of the time, meant to represent risk and the fragility of human accomplishment.

Paintings on this subject were often accompanied by verses with a moral, but what is the moral with respect to investing?

Moral: If you are the first in and the first out, Ponzi schemes are an excellent investment.

The Miser

Once upon a time there was a Miser who never spent his gold. He buried the gold in a secret hole in his garden. Every day he would dig it up and look at it.

"I'm so rich. I own all this gold!" he would chortle to himself.

But a passer-by saw him admiring his gold and decided to dig it up that night.

The next morning, the Miser came to look at his gold. His gold was gone!

"Who stole my gold?" he cried.

All the neighbors came running. He told them the story. "Did you ever spend any of your gold?" they asked. He answered, "No, I just liked looking at it."

Moral: If you can't buy anything with your money, it's worthless.

The Milkmaid and the Milk

A Milkmaid had milked the cows and was returning with the full milk pail balanced nicely on her head.

"This good, rich milk," she mused, "will give me plenty of cream to churn. The butter I make I will take to market, and with the money I will buy a lot of eggs for hatching. How nice it will be when they are all hatched and the yard is full of fine young chicks. I will sell them, and I'll buy a lovely new dress to wear to the fair. All the young men will admire me and want to marry me.

She tossed her head, and down fell the pail and all the milk flowed out. She cried over her lost prospects.

Moral: Don't count your chickens before they're hatched.

Sarah The Simple and Ada the Smart

Sarah advertised in a newspaper far and wide: "I can spin hair into gold."

People thought she was nuts.

Ada, on the other hand, wrote an article for a scientific journal. In very technical language, she described how, through the chemical action of various dyes, she could make a dye all on her own, to dye hair gold.

Word got out and the whole countryside flocked to Ada's door.

Moral: Beware fancy talk.

The Tortoise and the Hare

The Tortoise and the Hare were friends. When they were teenagers, they made a bet to see who would be richer by age 35.

The Hare was very smart and bought a lot of bitcoin. His bitcoin went up and up and at age 30 he was a millionaire.

The Tortoise became a plumber and worked very hard. He made good money but invested it all back into the plumbing company that he eventually owned. At age 30, he was CEO of his growing plumbing company but had no spare cash.

Then the price of bitcoin crashed.

At age 35, the Hare was bankrupt. The Tortoise was doing very well; plumbing was much in demand.

Moral: Slow and steady wins the race.

The Proud Man's New Clothes

There was once a Proud Man who was constantly looking for novel gadgets and new ways of doing things. He badly wanted a new set of clothes made of new fabrics and sewn in a novel way.

Two Tailors were summoned and, after thinking for a long time, they said: We could make you a set of new clothes with fabrics no one in this town has ever seen. They will be unbelievably beautiful and also magical.

"Magical in what way?" asked the man.

The Tailors replied, "Magical in that only the very clever can see them. The fabrics are invisible to most men. They can be appreciated only by those who are very clever. The process is very, very complicated. The process is called blockchain. The fabrics are sewn by decentralized computers from all over the world. They computers use a lot of energy so a suit costs around $20,000 – but that is a huge discount. Others have bought such suits for $69,000."

"Never mind the cost. You only live once," said the man. "I must have it. When can I have it? I'm ready to pay."

"You are wise," said the Tailors. "The suit will go up in value because it will be very rare. You'll be able to resell it next year for many times the amount. The price will be 'to the moon.'"

The Tailors worked very hard for several weeks and brought the new suit to the man wrapped in a very fancy box. When they opened the box, they oohed and aahed because the suit was so beautiful. "Try it on," they said, "but handle it gently because the fabric is very fine."

The man could not see anything in the box. "What color is it?" he asked.

"Can't you see, sir?" asked the Tailors. "It is a color that has no name because nothing like it has ever before been made. But since you are smart and understand technology, the true color will emerge for you as you look closely."

The man saw nothing no matter how closely he looked but he didn't want them to think that the suit was invisible to him so he pretended to be very pleased. "Ah," he said. "I see it now, it's truly magnificent."

The Tailors helped him to put it on and he gave them a $20,000 cheque which they quickly went to the bank to cash.

The man walked out on the street in his new clothes, proclaiming, "I am wearing a suit made of new colors and new fabrics by computers that use blockchain. To see my suit, you have to be very clever."

Everyone on the street first gulped, then applauded and cried out, "What a beautiful suit!"

But a wide-eyed child asked out loud, "What's with the naked guy?"

Moral: If you can't understand it, don't believe it.

The Boy Who Cried Wolf

When the Boy Shepherd wanted attention, he yelled. "Come quick, a Wolf has come to eat up my sheep!"

His friend dropped everything and came running, but it was all a hoax.

The trick worked so well, he did it again the next day. He cried "Wolf!" again for fun, and the friend came running again.

Then the Wolf really did come. The Boy cried out, "Wolf!"

Nobody came. The Wolf ate the sheep... and the Boy.

Moral: Fool me once shame on you. Fool me twice, shame on me. Fool me three times, and you are the *greater* fool.

The Whale and the Fish

A Whale and a Fish were swimming in the sea. "Ha, Ha," said the Whale. "I am so much bigger than you. I can take advantage of you in so many ways."

"You're not that big," said the Fish. "I've seen much bigger than you – but I know a way you can be the biggest."

"How?" asked the Whale.

"By swallowing a lot of hot air," said the Fish.

The Whale wanted to be the biggest so it swallowed more and more hot air until it exploded.

Moral: Just because a Whale is big doesn't make him smart.

The Card Shark and the Fool

The Card Shark and the Fool were playing cards.

The Fool was lucky and won a lot of money but he got greedy and kept right on playing until he lost it all.

**Moral: You have got to know when to hold 'em,
know when to fold 'em,
know when to walk away, know when to run.**

The Boy and the Cookies

A Boy put his hand in the cookie jar and drew out a delicious cookie.

Not satisfied, he took two more.

They were so good that he decided to grab a handful but, with all those cookies in his hand, he got stuck, had to go to hospital to get his hand pulled out safely, and ate no cookies.

Moral: Be satisfied with a little lest you're left with nothing.

The Country Mouse and the Town Mouse

The Country Mouse envied his cousin, the Town Mouse, because of all the delicacies available in town, all the luxuries of urban life, all the concerts, and museums, and lavish parties.

He couldn't wait to visit his cousin. But, as soon as he arrived, he was chased by his cousin's cat and terrorized by his cousin's dog. He swiftly returned home and said to his wife, "There's no place like home."

Moral: Be happy with what you have.

The Lion and the Asses

Everyone paid respect to the wise old Lion, the king of the beasts. Everyone, that is, except the young Asses. They brayed in a scornful way whenever the Lion passed.

How best to respond, thought the Lion. "Should I hold them up to ridicule?"

He decided to ignore them.

Moral: Ignoring an insult can be powerful.

The Oak and the Reeds

The Oak and the Reeds argued about strategy.

The Oak thought it was best to stand up against headwinds; the Reeds thought it was best to bow low.

A great hurricane came and proved the Reeds right. The storm was so great that the strong Oak fell but the Reeds, as always, fared well.

Moral: Adapt or die.

The Little Wolf and His Mother

The Little Wolf saw a lot of bright shining bitcoins advertised on TV. He tried to get at them but only shattered the glass of the TV screen and was punished by Mother Wolf.

Then the Little Wolf heard his father's friends boasting about their amazing bitcoin gains and he started to howl that he wanted some too. But the men only laughed at him.

His feelings hurt, he said, "I don't want them anyway. They're no good. They'll melt in your hand. They're not worth it. They're good for nothing."

The men laughed and said, "Sour grapes!" But summer came, and the bitcoin melted. The Little Wolf had been right.

Moral: Sour grapes may well be sour.

The Wolf and the Crane

A Wolf got a bone stuck in his throat so he hurried to the Crane and asked her to pull it out for him with her long beak .

"If you do it, I will reward you very handsomely," the Wolf said.

Greedy for a reward, the Crane did as she was asked.

"What about my reward!" said the Crane. "Ah," said the Wolf, "You remember when you put your beak in my mouth?"

"Yes," said the Crane. "Well, I was going to bite it off. But I didn't. That was your reward."

Moral: Be grateful you lost only half your money rather than all.

The Ass and His Driver

An Ass was being driven along a road when he suddenly saw something golden that sparkled very brightly over the edge of the cliff. He lunged for it.

Just as he was about to leap over, his master caught him by the tail and tried to pull him back from disaster, but the stubborn Ass would not yield.

"I give up," said the driver. "Do what you must."

The foolish Ass pushed ahead, went over the cliff, tried to hold on for dear life, but tumbled to his death.

Moral: Listen to good advice.

The Sheep and the Pig

A Shepherd one day caught a Pig and started off to the butcher's.

The Pig squealed at the top of its voice.

"Why are you squealing?" asked the Sheep. "The Shepherd regularly catches us and takes us off somewhere. We don't make a fuss."

"That is all very well," replied the Pig. "When he catches you he is only after your wool. But, with me, he wants my bacon!"

**Moral: The rich can afford to be taken for a ride.
The poor can't.**

The Wolves and the Wolverine

Mr. Wolf was hungry so he stole the food that the Wolverine had saved for her babies.

The next day, while the Wolf was out hunting, the Wolverine stole back from the Wolf.

Moral: There's no honor among thieves.

The Deer and His Shadow

A Deer looking at his huge shadow felt he was a hundred times bigger than he was.

He thought he was the king of the beasts. So he lingered looking at his shadow.

He learned his lesson when a lion ate him up.

Moral: Pride goeth before a fall.

The Ass in the Lion's Skin

An Ass found a lion's skin left in the forest, dressed himself in it, and had a great time frightening all the animals that passed by. They were awed by him and frightened. The Fox fled and hid behind a tree.

The Ass was so pleased with himself, that he let out a loud, harsh bray. Hearing the bray, the Fox laughed. "You've given yourself away!" he said.

Moral: You can dress fancy but something will give you away.

The Fisher and the Little Fish

A poor Fisher was having no luck catching fish but, at the end of the day, he caught a very Small Fish.

"Please," said the Small Fish, "throw me back in the water. I am so small, I'm not worth anything. Put me back and catch me again when I am grown."

"No," said the Fisher, "better small than nothing at all."

Moral: Small sure gains are better than grand hopes.

The Fighting Cocks and the Eagle

There were two Cocks who were rivals and fought with each other.

One day, one of the Cocks had a decisive victory. He was so proud of himself that he flew to the top of the henhouse and crowed with delight.

An Eagle who was flying overhead noticed him, swooped down and carried him off.

Moral: With great ignorance comes great confidence.
With great confidence comes great danger.

The Wolves and the Sheep

A pack of Wolves were hungry for sheep but the guard Dogs kept them away.

The clever Wolves said to the Sheep, "You don't need those middlemen Dogs. Why don't you get rid of them and deal directly with us? We're your friends."

The Sheep thought that was a good idea since it would give them more freedom to roam. They didn't see the need for middlemen. So they sent the Dogs away.

And the Wolves had a great feast.

Moral: Beware self-interested advice.

The Lion and the Hare

The Lion chased all horned creatures out of his territory because their horns were dangerous.

One day the Lion saw a Hare's shadow in the early morning sunshine, which made the Hare's innocent ears look like long horns. The Lion gobbled him up.

Moral: Appearances can be deceiving.

The Miller, His Son, and the Ass

One day, an old Miller and his son went to market with an Ass they hoped to sell. They wanted him in good condition so they walked carefully with the Ass at their side.

Along came a passer-by who said, "What foolishness to walk when you can ride."

The Miller took this to heart and told his son to climb on the Ass.

Soon they met another passer-by who said, "There's no respect for age anymore. The young ride and the old suffer."

The Miller thought he had been wrong and changed places with his son.

But the next passer-by thought the opposite. "Look at that old guy riding in style while the poor boy trudges along."

The Miller then asked the Boy to climb up on the Ass beside him.

But the next passer-by was horrified. "Look at those two taking advantage of the poor animal."

The Miller and his son quickly scrambled down, slung the Ass from a pole and carried him to market. But no one would buy the animal because they thought it was too ill to walk.

Moral: Think for yourself.

The Little Boy

There was a Boy who was very indulged by his parents.

When he got a new toy, he cried because it wasn't what he expected. When his parents bought him a present of bitcoin, he cried because he could only see a picture of the bitcoin; he couldn't play with them.

When he heard that adults were playing with bitcoin, he howled and howled with anger. He yelled at the adults, "Bitcoin is nothing." But no one listened. No one paid attention until the day they lost their holdings.

Moral: Children know what is real.

The Boy and the Balloon

Freddie, age 5, accidentally let go of the large balloon he had bought at the fair.

He cried and cried but his father comforted him, "What goes up, Freddie, must always come down."

Moral: Bubbles rise but soon deflate.

The Elephant and the Squirrel

An Elephant and a Squirrel decided to go skating on the pond.

Along with his skates, the Elephant put on a large pillow tied around his middle. "What's that for?" asked the Squirrel.

"So that I don't hurt so much when I fall," answered the Elephant.

Moral: The bigger they are, the harder they fall.

Julie and Millie

Julie and Millie were twin sisters. Julie became a famous violinist and Millie resented it.

"How come you and not me,?" Millie said to her sister.

"Well," said Julie, "I spent all the free time I had growing up practising the violin. You spent all your free time playing with your friends."

Moral: There is no shortcut to success.

The Wolf and the Naïve Shepherd

A Wolf had a scheme.

He told the Shepherd that all he had to do was to leave the sheep hatch open so he could come in and turn sheep wool into gold. He could make the Shepherd very rich.

The Wolf did come in and ate the sheep, but left no gold.

Moral: Beware false promises.

The Tale of Two Lemonade Stands

Perry and Jerry were friends who lived on the same street.

Perry set up a lemonade stand outside his house on a hot summer day and business was lively.

He said to his friend, Jerry, "Why don't you set up one too?"

Jerry thought it was a great idea and set up his stand just up the street in the exact same way.

What Perry couldn't figure out was why his business suddenly went sour.

Moral: In a zero-sum game, what one person wins, another must lose.

The Apologetic Leopard

A bad Leopard who kept eating Farmer Smith's chickens was caught and sent to jail.

He confessed and repented and apologized over and over to Farmer Smith.

Farmer Smith was a kind man and paid bail for the Leopard so the Leopard could go home to his leopard family.

The next day, what do you think happened? The Leopard ate more chickens than ever; he was so hungry after his stint in jail.

Moral: A leopard does not change its spots.

The Oxen and the Wheels

A pair of Oxen were drawing a heavy wagon along a muddy road. It was hard. They had to use all their strength to pull the wagon, but they did not complain. They did what they had to do.

The wheels, on the other hand, who really did not have to exert themselves too much since the Oxen were doing all the work, moaned and groaned at every turn. Their complaints made it all the harder for the Oxen to concentrate on their heavy task.

Moral: The least hard-working complain the most about their lot in life.

The Plane Tree

Two Travellers, walking in the noon day sun, were hot and tired and decided to lie down on the grass in the shade of a large, leafy plane tree.

One said to the other, "Look at this tree and all its leaves! It never bears fruit, just litters the ground with leaves. How useless!"

Moral: Give credit to structures that protect us from ourselves (the law, financial institutions and governments).

The Farmer and the Stork

A Stork, honest and trusting, accepted an invitation from the Cranes for a party on a newly planted field.

The Cranes ate the Farmer's seeds and the Farmer's revenge was to entrap them all, including the Stork, in a great big net. The party ended dismally with all the birds entangled in the mesh of the Farmer's net.

"Please let me go," pleaded the Stork. "I belong to the stork family who are honest birds. I have never stolen anything in my life."

"You may be a very good bird," answered the Farmer, "but you keep bad company."

Moral: You're judged by the friends you keep.

The Travelers and the Purse

Two Travelers were walking along a country road when one of them picked up a purse well-filled with government-printed currency.

"How lucky *I* am!" he said.

Just then there was a shout of "Stop, thief!" A mob of people armed with clubs were coming down the road.

"**We** are lost," cried the man who had found the purse, changing pronouns, "if they find **our** purse."

Moral: Risk takers like to keep profits for themselves but spread losses amongst many.

The Dog and the Bone

A very hungry Dog found a bone in a butcher shop. He was overjoyed and decided to take it to a secret place in the woods to enjoy it in privacy.

He had to cross a river and, while hopping from stone to stone, he looked down and saw his reflection in the water.

What he saw was a dog holding a bone which looked bigger than the one he had. So he opened his jaws to grab the bigger bone and, of course, his own bone fell in the river and sank.

Moral: Greed gets you in trouble.

The Thirsty Fox

There was a Fox walking in the hot sun, very thirsty. He saw a well and wanted to drink from it. As he tried, he fell in.

"How will I get out?" he asked himself.

Just then, a Goat passed by and saw him in the well. "Hey, Fox, what are you doing in the well?" asked the Goat.

"I just came in to cool myself off," said the Fox. "It's so hot, why don't you come in too?"

The Goat jumped in and swam around. "But how will we get out?" he asked.

The Fox said, "Why don't you stand on your hind legs and I'll climb on you and get out that way."

The Goat obligingly did that. "Now, how shall I get out?" he asked.

"You should have thought of that before" laughed the Fox as he departed.

Moral: Be sure to know if you are partners or competitors.

The Old Lion and the Fox

An old Lion was very weak and could no longer hunt. But he figured out a way to survive.

He told a Bird to spread the news in the jungle that he was dying and was writing his will. He asked the Bird to tell all the animals to visit him in his den, one by one, to see what he was leaving them in his will and to say goodbye.

The Bird did as she was told and, one by one, the animals came to visit the Lion, and, one by one, he caught them and ate them.

The last to approach was the Fox, who waited at the opening to the Lion's den.

"Come in, Fox," roared the Lion, "I have something special for you because you are the foxiest."

"I am sorry you are ill, Lion," said the Fox, but I'm not coming in."

"Why not?" asked the Lion.

The Fox replied, "Because all the footprints outside the den, and there are many, are going *in*, and I don't see any going *out!*"

Moral: Look at the evidence.

Jack and the Beanstalk

Once upon a time, there lived a mother and her little son Jack. They lived together on a small farm with one cow.

On the brink of a dire financial situation, Jack's mother told him to go sell their cow at the market. But Jack was tired. He didn't want to walk all the way to market, even if he would receive a handsome fee.

His luck changed, though, when on the way to market, a well-dressed fellow came up to Jack and offered him "the deal of his life": one Bitcoin for his cow.

"The cow is worth $20,000," the man told Jack. "You wouldn't sell her for nearly that much at the market."

The man's suit and confident demeanor told Jack that this was a guy to trust. And one Bitcoin was worth $20,000! Inflation really hasn't hit this currency.

So Jack traded the cow for the Bitcoin and headed back home.

"Ma, Ma" Jack cried. "I got us the deal of the century."

"What great news! How much money did you get for her?" Jack's mother waited excitingly to hear.

"Money!?" Jack laughed. "I got something much better than that – Bitcoin."

So Jack proceeded to tell his mother about this fabulous new-fangled invention that really was worth more than gold! Jack's mother went through the five stages of grief right in front of him. Jack was confused by his mother's crying.

Jack remembered that the well-dressed man told him that Bitcoin would show you its worth if you let it. So Jack set the Bitcoin down in the field and waited to see what would happen. Patience, Jack remembered. So he went to bed, stuffing a pillow over his head to soothe the noise of his crying mother. Her cries, he knew, would soon turn to tears of joy.

The next morning, Jack ran excitingly back out to the field. Sure enough, the well-dressed man was right. Right before Jack, instead of the Bitcoin, was a giant beanstalk. If this was any regular beanstalk, Jack may have been disappointed, but Jack could see the Bitcoin logo all over this beanstalk, so knew that it must be legit.

As any curious young adventurer would, Jack started to climb. Up and up the Bitcoin beanstalk he went, following the logo, his eyes glowing more with each step.

Jack could hardly believe what he saw when he finally made it over the mist and into the clouds. It was a land full of Bitcoin. Large Bitcoin, small Bitcoin, it was all there!

Barely able to believe his luck, Jack hurriedly started shoving Bitcoin into his satchel. With each Bitcoin he collected, his smile grew just thinking about how happy his mother would be.

There was one particularly shiny Bitcoin that caught his eye. He reached down to grab it when, all of a sudden, a giant thunder rolled through the Bitcoin land.

"Fee-fi-fo-fum. Leave the Bitcoin before I come. Come and drag you by the hair to my feet, where I will feast on you, sweet treat." Jack looked up to see these words coming from a giant creature as tall as a windmill, standing in front of him.

The creature's head was round, his eyes set wide with eyebrows high on his head, and his mouth curved tightly into a smile. Even without squinting, Jack could see that the features carved a giant "B" onto his face. Could this be? The Bitcoin King?

Jack's feet were telling him to run, but his mind urged him to stay. What about all of the Bitcoin that he would leave behind? Jack grabbed the shiny Bitcoin by his feet and kept running around, picking up some more.

The Bitcoin King was unimpressed, sending another thunder down the gold-plated valley. Jack, however, could not be pulled from his daze. Entranced in his search for the best Bitcoin, Jack did not notice as the Bitcoin King began to run down the valley towards him. Nor did Jack notice as the Bitcoin King's giant shadow loomed on the ground in front. It was only when the Bitcoin King finally reached Jack and grabbed him by the hair that Jack took notice.

All of a sudden, in a state of shock, Jack scrambled as quickly as he could out of the creature's grasp. He kicked the creature in the chin and jumped down to the ground. Jack sprinted back through the Bitcoins and onto the beanstalk. He slid down quickly at a speed too great for the creature to follow behind. When he finally reached the bottom, Jack slid into the ground with a big thud, the contents of his bag spilling outwards.

The pain that Jack felt in his back was soothed by the realization that he still had all of his Bitcoin, ten to be exact.

"What a deal!" Jack exclaimed. "Now, mother and I have $200,000."

He soon felt his stomach churn, though, as he again heard the pained cries of his mother in the house. While Jack longed to hold onto the shiny Bitcoin, he knew that it would make his mother so happy if he brought $200,000 in real cash back home. What a life it would bring them!

So Jack gathered the Bitcoin up and set off to sell them. He couldn't help but remark that the Bitcoin appeared less shiny in his bag than it had when he first saw it.

Jack spent the rest of the afternoon walking along the trail, looking for the well-dressed man. He stopped a few passers-by on the trail to ask them if he had seen him.

"He was wearing a suit and had a striking air of confidence," Jack relayed.

"Might you mean the Milk Man?" One of the passers-by inquired. "He wears a suit, is quite confident, and also sells the best milk in all of the land."

The passer-by pulled out a canteen from his bag filled with creamy, thick milk. Jack took a sip and agreed that this was some of the best milk that he had ever tasted.

"I don't think that this man sold milk, but I sure would like to get some of this. So if you could point me in the direction of him, I would appreciate it."

So the passer-by pointed Jack in the right direction, and off he went.

After walking for some time, he saw what looked to be the suited man in the distance milking the very cow that Jack had sold to him.

"Sir, sir." Jack cried, racing over to him. "I wish to sell my Bitcoin back. And, look, I have ten of them now."

"Now, why would you want to do such a thing?" the man asked.

"To get money for my mother and me. She has been crying all day because we have no money."

"I can help you out with that then." The man said with a wide smile. "I will buy them, with real money, for their worth."

"Oh, thank you, sir." Jack replied, "You don't know how happy this will make my mother."

The man opened his cash register, and Jack placed the Bitcoin on the table in front of him. The man took the Bitcoin, turned, and went back to milking the cow.

Jack, confused at this man's priorities in such a dire time for Jack, slammed the table hard.

"Hey. You need to give me my money."

"I agreed to pay you what the Bitcoin are worth, and I have."

Jack was concerned at this man's obvious stupidity.

"No," Jack said slowly as if talking to a child. "Each Bitcoin is worth $20,000. That is what you said when I paid for the Bitcoin by handing over the cow to you."

The man shook his head.

"That is what it was worth yesterday, yes, but today it is worth nothing."

Jack's cheeks grew so red his hair looked white.

"Here," the man said. "Have a glass of milk, I am selling so much here that I have more than enough to give away for free. People will always need milk, so this cow here will always have value. Thanks for her, she will do me well."

With that, the man got up and walked into his large mansion, leaving Jack fuming.

Without any more options, Jack turned to trudge home, dejected, embarrassed and scared about his and his mother's future.

He kicked the dirt along the path as he walked, watching it fly up into the air and back down again. On one particular kick, the dirt flying up did not look like dirt at all, but beans. He bent down to pick up the beans. He looked them over; just ordinary beans, nothing special. How great it would be to eat a bean for dinner, Jack thought. As his stomach growled, he thought back to what the crooked man had said.

"People will always need milk, so this cow here will always have value."

"And people will always need beans!" Jack picked up all the beans in sight and ran back home.

Three years later, Jack's house was the place to be. Farmers came from all over to buy Jack's famous beans, and Jack and his mother no longer thought of hunger or cold. It was hard work farming all of the beans, but Jack had since learned his lesson.

Moral: Taking shortcuts just makes the trip longer.

Printed in Great Britain
by Amazon

33136999R00066